THERE ONCE WAS A VERY odd SCHOOL

and other lunch-box limericks

by
Stephen Krensky

illustrated by
Tamara Petrosino

DUTTON CHILDREN'S BOOKS · NEW YORK

CIP Data is available.

Published in the United States 2004 by Dutton Children's Books,
a division of Penguin Young Readers Group
345 Hudson Street, New York, New York 10014
www.penguin.com

Designed by Richard Amari

Manufactured in China
First Edition
ISBN 0-525-46974-5
1 3 5 7 9 10 8 6 4 2

There once was a very odd school
That had only one little rule:
There was recess all day
To learn best how to play,
Which everyone thought was so cool.

The talent show makes me real nervous.
So many will come to observe us.

If I get too intense
And lose confidence,

I'll put myself
right out of service.

Nicole drew a dragon in art,
which breathed fire right from the start.
Then she drew a brave knight,
which it wanted to fight,
So she had to keep them apart.

Nick stares at his food tray in fear.
He wonders what's happening here.
Spaghetti that wriggles?
And Jell-O that giggles?
He might just skip lunch for the year.

The principal sees through my brain
Like an X-ray machine gone insane.
It's not really my fault.
I did try to say "Halt!"
After launching the big paper plane.

There's a kid who's giving me trouble.
He'd like to reduce me to rubble.
If I do blow my stack,
I might just fight back,
But I sure wish that I were a double.

If I'm ever picked first for a team,
I know I'll let out a big scream.
I'll pinch myself twice—
A small sacrifice—
To make sure that it isn't a dream.

The new kid at school seems so shy,
He can barely mumble out "Hi!"

But once down in gym,

SLAM

GOAL

There's no stopping him.

MOVE!

MOVE!

MOVE!

In sports he's a very loud guy.

The lunch lady fills her tureen now,
But no one has ever just seen how.
Her secret ingredient
She adds when expedient,

which explains why I have turned green now.

I ran down the hall to the nurse,
Feeling like I was under a curse.
"It's not a bad case,"
She said with a straight face.

"Bright stripes would be horribly worse."

Why can't my new school bus be red,

Like a big fire engine or sled?

Yellow's so boring,
I go to school snoring

And wish I was home in my bed.

The substitute stands up before us.
I know that she's going to bore us.
   It would just be so great
   If she'd simply mutate
Into a tyrannosaurus.

To learn spelling is such a big grind.
I'm constantly falling behind.
    I hate *i* before *e*
    Except after *c*.
Why can't *i* just make up its mind?

A nervous young student named Janet
Has a teacher not from our planet.
The last students who gabbed
During one science lab
Are now statues made out of granite.

The problem with sneakers is laces
That flop all around in most places.
It's not really much fun
If they just come undone
When I'm busy rounding the bases.

Class pictures can be a disaster.
The photo guy's such a taskmaster.
    He tells us, "Say *cheese!*
    And please do not sneeze!*"
I wish that he took them much faster.

Alexander liked learning to add,
And subtracting—it wasn't so bad,
   But multiplication
   Was full of frustration.
Big numbers just made him so mad!

Have you heard the story of Mabel,
Who wanted to learn the times table?
    She struggled, alas,
    But will come back to class,
Though not until Mabel is able.

While it may not help much to complain,
I think homework is quite a big pain.
First the teachers define it,
And then they assign it.

That's too much of a strain for my brain.

At lunch as we gobble our food,
One person makes sure we're not rude.
    As he wanders each aisle,
    He rarely does smile.
He stays in a serious mood.

When making a class presentation,
I don't get a standing ovation.
While I do all my talking,
My knees keep on knocking,
And after, I need a vacation.

In music class Jill's very proud
To sing out both boldly and loud.
   But the crack in her throat
   When she hits a high note
Makes her really stand out from the crowd.

Marie had a hamster that nicked her,

And Justin's white rabbit just licked her,

But my teacher said "**NO!**"
When I brought in to show
My brand-new pet boa constrictor.

Hooray for the summer at last!
The school year is all in the past.
It feels great to be free,
But between you and me,

The next one will get here too fast.